FOR ALL LITTLE FRIENDS OF
MR. McGREGOR & PETER & BENJAMIN

Frederick Warne has a continuing commitment to reproduce Beatrix Potter's exquisite watercolours to the highest possible standard. In 1993 and 1994, taking advantage of the latest advances in printing technology and expertise, entirely new film was made from her original book illustrations. The drawings are now reproduced with a quality and a degree of authenticity never before attainable in print.

FREDERICK WARNE

Published by the Penguin Group
27 Wrights Lane, London W8 5TZ, England
Penguin Books USA Inc., 375 Hudson Street, New York, N.Y. 10014, USA
Penguin Books Australia Ltd, Ringwood, Victoria, Australia
Penguin Books Canada Ltd, 10 Alcorn Avenue, Toronto, Ontario, Canada M4V 3B2
Penguin Books (N.Z.) Ltd, 182-190 Wairau Road, Auckland 10, New Zealand

Penguin Books Ltd, Registered Offices: Harmondsworth, Middlesex, England

First published 1909 by Frederick Warne
This edition with new reproductions of Beatrix Potter's book illustrations first
published 1996

This edition copyright © Frederick Warne & Co. 1996
New reproductions copyright © Frederick Warne & Co., 1995
Original copyright in text and illustrations © Frederick Warne & Co., 1909

Frederick Warne & Co. is the owner of all rights, copyrights and trademarks in the
Beatrix Potter character names and illustrations.

All rights reserved. Without limiting the rights under copyright reserved above, no
part of this publication may be reproduced, stored in or introduced into a retrieval
system, or transmitted, in any form or by any means (electronic, mechanical,
photocopying, recording or otherwise), without the prior written permission of the
above publisher of this book.

Colour reproduction by
Saxon Photolitho Ltd, Norwich
Printed and bound in Great Britain by
William Clowes Limited, Beccles and London

THE TALE OF THE
FLOPSY BUNNIES

❃

BY BEATRIX POTTER

F. WARNE & CO.

IT is said that the effect of eating too much lettuce is "soporific".

I have never felt sleepy after eating lettuces; but then *I* am not a rabbit.

They certainly had a very soporific effect upon the Flopsy Bunnies!

WHEN Benjamin Bunny grew up, he married his Cousin Flopsy. They had a large family, and they were very improvident and cheerful.

I do not remember the separate names of their children; they were generally called the "Flopsy Bunnies".

AS there was not always quite enough to eat, Benjamin used to borrow cabbages from Flopsy's brother, Peter Rabbit, who kept a nursery garden.

SOMETIMES
Peter Rabbit had
no cabbages to
spare.

When this
happened, the
Flopsy Bunnies
went across the
field to a rubbish
heap, in the ditch
outside Mr.
McGregor's garden.

MR. McGregor's rubbish heap was a mixture. There were jam pots and paper bags, and mountains of chopped grass from the mowing machine (which always tasted oily), and some rotten vegetable marrows and an old boot or two. One day—oh joy!—there were a quantity of overgrown lettuces, which had "shot" into flower.

THE Flopsy Bunnies simply stuffed lettuces.
By degrees, one after another, they were
overcome with slumber, and lay down in the
mown grass.

Benjamin was not so much overcome as his
children. Before going to sleep he was
sufficiently wide awake to put a paper bag
over his head to keep off the flies.

THE little Flopsy Bunnies slept delightfully
in the warm sun. From the lawn beyond the
garden came the distant clacketty sound of
the mowing machine. The bluebottles buzzed
about the wall, and a little old mouse picked
over the rubbish among the jam pots.

(I can tell you her name, she was called
Thomasina Tittlemouse, a woodmouse with a
long tail.)

SHE rustled across the paper bag, and awakened Benjamin Bunny.

The mouse apologized profusely, and said that she knew Peter Rabbit.

WHILE she and Benjamin were talking, close under the wall, they heard a heavy tread above their heads; and suddenly Mr. McGregor emptied out a sackful of lawn mowings right upon the top of the sleeping Flopsy Bunnies! Benjamin shrank down under his paper bag. The mouse hid in a jam pot.

THE little rabbits smiled sweetly in their sleep under the shower of grass; they did not awake because the lettuces had been so soporific.

They dreamt that their mother Flopsy was tucking them up in a hay bed.

Mr. McGregor looked down after emptying his sack. He saw some funny little brown tips of ears sticking up through the lawn mowings. He stared at them for some time.

PRESENTLY a fly
settled on one of
them and it moved.

Mr. McGregor
climbed down on to
the rubbish heap—
"One, two, three,
four! five! six leetle
rabbits!" said he as
he dropped them
into his sack.

The Flopsy Bunnies dreamt that their mother
was turning them over in bed. They stirred a
little in their sleep, but still they did not wake
up.

Mr. McGregor tied up the sack and left it on
the wall.

He went to put away the mowing machine.

WHILE he was gone, Mrs. Flopsy Bunny
(who had remained at home) came across the
field.

She looked suspiciously at the sack and
wondered where everybody was?

THEN the mouse came out of her jam pot, and Benjamin took the paper bag off his head, and they told the doleful tale.

Benjamin and Flopsy were in despair, they could not undo the string.

But Mrs. Tittlemouse was a resourceful person. She nibbled a hole in the bottom corner of the sack.

THE little rabbits were pulled out and
pinched to wake them.

Their parents stuffed the empty sack with
three rotten vegetable marrows, an old
blacking-brush and two decayed turnips.

THEN they all hid under a bush and watched for Mr. McGregor.

Mr. McGregor came back and picked up the sack, and carried it off.

He carried it hanging down, as if it were rather heavy.

The Flopsy Bunnies followed at a safe distance.

THEY watched him go into his house.
  And then they crept up to the window to
listen.

MR. McGREGOR threw down the sack on the stone floor in a way that would have been extremely painful to the Flopsy Bunnies, if they had happened to have been inside it.

They could hear him drag his chair on the flags, and chuckle—

"One, two, three, four, five, six leetle rabbits!" said Mr. McGregor.

"EH? What's that? What have they been spoiling now?" enquired Mrs. McGregor.

"One, two, three, four, five, six leetle fat rabbits!" repeated Mr. McGregor, counting on his fingers—

"one, two, three—"

"Don't you be silly; what do you mean, you silly old man?"

"In the sack! one, two, three, four, five, six!" replied Mr. McGregor.

(The youngest Flopsy Bunny got upon the window-sill.)

MRS. McGREGOR took hold of the sack and felt it. She said she could feel six, but they must be *old* rabbits, because they were so hard and all different shapes.

"Not fit to eat; but the skins will do fine to line my old cloak."

"Line your old cloak?" shouted Mr. McGregor—"I shall sell them and buy myself baccy!"

"Rabbit tobacco! I shall skin them and cut off their heads."

MRS. McGREGOR untied the sack and put
her hand inside.

When she felt the vegetables she became
very very angry. She said that Mr. McGregor
had "done it a purpose."

AND Mr. McGregor was very angry too.
One of the rotten marrows came flying
through the kitchen window, and hit the
youngest Flopsy Bunny.
  It was rather hurt.

THEN Benjamin and Flopsy thought that it was time to go home.

SO Mr. McGregor did not get his tobacco, and Mrs. McGregor did not get her rabbit skins.

But next Christmas Thomasina Tittlemouse got a present of enough rabbit-wool to make herself a cloak and a hood, and a handsome muff and a pair of warm mittens.